21st Century Skills Library

GLOBAL PERSPECTIVES

GENETICALLY MODIFIED FOODS

Vicky Franchino

Cherry Lake Publishing
Ann Arbor, Michigan

CHERRY
LAKE
Publishing

Published in the United States of America by Cherry Lake Publishing
Ann Arbor, Michigan
www.cherrylakepublishing.com

Content Adviser: Dr. Arpad Pusztai, Norwegian Institute of Genetic Ecology, Aberdeen, Scotland

Photo Credits: Cover and page 1, © Christopher Elwell, used under license from Shutterstock, Inc.; page 4, © salamanderman, used under license from Shutterstock, Inc.; page 6, © Sean Sprague/Alamy; page 8, © Deco Images/Alamy; page 9, © iStockphoto. com/kickers; page 11, © Custom Medical Stock Photo/Alamy; page 12, © Peter Arnold, Inc./Alamy; pages 14 and 26, © David Hoffman Photo Library/Alamy; page 17, © Wieslaw Fila, used under license from Shutterstock, Inc.; page 18, © Shi Yali, used under license from Shutterstock, Inc.; page 21, © Holt Studios International Ltd/Alamy; page 22, © Patrick Hermans, used under license from Shutterstock, Inc.; page 24, © Chad Ehlers/Alamy; page 25, © iStockphoto.com/sjlocke

Map by XNR Productions Inc.

Library of Congress Cataloging-in-Publication Data
Franchino, Vicky.
Genetically modified food / by Vicky Franchino.
    p. cm.—(Global perspectives)
Includes index.
ISBN-13: 978-1-60279-132-9
ISBN-10: 1-60279-132-5
1. Genetically modified foods—Juvenile literature. I. Title. II. Series.
TP248.65.F66F757 2008
664—dc22   2007038840

*Cherry Lake Publishing would like to acknowledge the work of
The Partnership for 21st Century Skills.
Please visit* www.21stcenturyskills.org *for more information.*

TABLE OF CONTENTS

CHAPTER ONE

READY TO DIG IN

You can't tell just by looking at them whether or not fruits and vegetables have been grown from genetically modified seeds.

As Charlie McEwan unpacked his bags, he came across a package his mother had slipped in when he wasn't looking. Eagerly tearing it open, he discovered a new comic book and a box of his favorite cookies. Absentmindedly reading the label as he helped himself to a snack, Charlie's eyes were drawn to the line "No genetically modified ingredients," on the back of the box. It was just like his mother to avoid anything made with what she called Frankenfoods. It was "organic or nothing" at their home in London. Last year, his mother had even taken him to a rally to protest genetically modified foods. It had been quite exciting!

Down the hall, Grace Foster, from Mason City, Iowa, was unpacking, too, while she chatted with her roommate, Miyanda Chona, from Lusaka, Zambia. All three of them were members of a group of students who had been invited to attend a meeting in Brussels, Belgium, where they would learn about genetically modified, or GM, foods.

Grace had never even heard of GM foods before she was invited to the meeting, but in the last few months she had tried to learn all she could. She had done some research on the Internet, gotten books from the library and talked to a farmer she knew who grew GM crops. "It's kind of weird," Grace told Miyanda. "I live in an area where we grow lots of genetically modified crops, but I bet I'm the only kid in my class who's even heard of genetically modified food."

Miyanda had first heard about GM food when Zambia had decided not to accept it from other countries. This food had been sent to feed

Food is distributed in Zambia during a famine.
Leaders in Zambia refused some food offered by other
countries because it was genetically modified.

people who didn't have enough to eat because of a famine, but the leaders

of her country weren't sure it was safe. At the time, this had seemed like

a good decision. The more Miyanda thought about it, however, the more

questions she had. She knew that people in the United States and Canada were eating genetically modified food, but that many people in Europe and Japan weren't. She also knew that a lot of empty plates could have been filled if her country had accepted the GM food. Would it have been better to take the risk? Miyanda hoped this conference would help answer some of her questions.

As Charlie, Grace, and Miyanda had already begun to learn, genetically modified food affects people around the world. It's a topic that many people have very strong opinions about, and that some people know almost nothing about—even if they're eating GM foods on a regular basis!

Learning & Innovation Skills

What is a genetically modified food? In general, it's a food, such as a vegetable or plant, which has had its genes changed in some way. But it can be a little trickier than that.

Some people say a food is only a GM food if it hasn't been processed. One example would be GM tomatoes sold in a grocery store. Others say that a GM food is anything that's made with any ingredients from genetically modified organisms. An example of this would be a cracker made with soybean oil that came from GM soybeans, even though all the genetic material is removed when the oil is processed. Using different definitions can make it hard to decide if a food should be considered a GM food.

If you were a leader in a country that banned GM foods, which definition would you use? What definition would you use if you owned a business that wanted to sell GM foods in a country that banned them?

CHAPTER TWO

STARTING AT THE GROUND LEVEL

*Scientists grow genetically modified plants in
labs and study their characteristics.*

The next morning, the students gathered in the main laboratory for a
lesson on how new foods are created. "We need to understand the basics
before we can have a discussion about genetic modification," said their
instructor, Dr. Ankur.

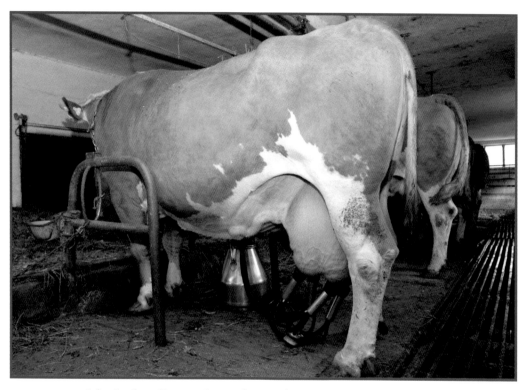

Selective breeding can be used to produce cows that give more milk.

The first thing Dr. Ankur told them was that making changes to plants and animals was something people had been doing for a long time. "If you had a potato or a piece of wheat from thousands of years ago, it would look nothing like those foods do today," he said. "Can anyone tell us about ways to change food?"

"I read about selection," said Grace. "It's when people only collect seeds from certain plants—maybe the ones that had bigger fruit—and use them to grow better plants the next year. You can do this with animals, too. For example, you could only breed the cows that have a characteristic you want, like giving more milk."

Hiro Ono, a boy from Tokyo, Japan, had heard of another method. "My aunt is a biologist, and she told me about crossbreeding. It's when you take different plants or animals and breed them with each other."

Genes are part of every living organism. But just what are genes? If you looked at one of your cells under a strong microscope, you'd see a nucleus in the center. Inside the nucleus you would see 46 chromosomes. All living things have chromosomes. There are different numbers for different types of organisms. There is a tiny package of deoxyribonucleic acid, more commonly known as DNA, inside each chromosome. The chemicals are in a certain order, a special sort of code. Each section of the code is a gene. A gene tells your body to make a certain protein. A protein tells your body to make or do something. Genes let one generation pass down characteristics to another. They're why you might be tall like your father or have red hair like your mom.

During the 1970s, researchers had their first success with genetic modification. They discovered an enzyme, a form of protein, that could be used like a chemical scissors to cut out a piece of DNA material in a cell.

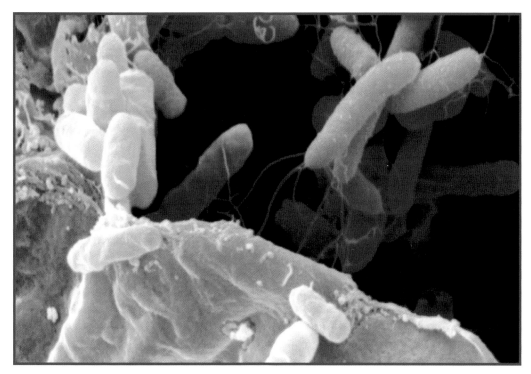

Agrobacterium tumefaciens *is used to transfer genetic material from one plant to another.*

Scientists used this enzyme to remove DNA from one cell and then put it into another. The result was called recombinant DNA, or rDNA.

With plants, scientists typically use one of two methods to create rDNA. One uses a type of bacterium, known as *Agrobacterium,* that lives in soil and can enter another plant's cells. First, scientists find the gene they want in one organism and add it to the *Agrobacterium.* Then they combine the changed *Agrobacterium* with cells from the plant that they

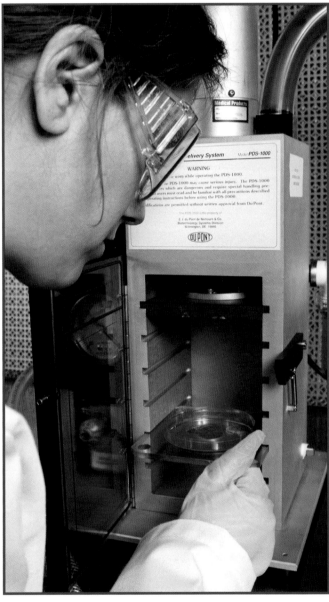

A scientist uses a gene gun to insert DNA from one plant into the cell of another plant.

want to add the new gene to. The scientists test the cells to see if the *Agrobacterium* has found its way in. If it has, then they grow plants from the successful cells.

Scientists can also insert DNA into a cell with a gene gun. They coat tiny balls of gold or magnesium-tungsten (a combination of metals) with genetic material and shoot them into a plant's cell.

Although these methods give scientists control over which genes are added into a plant, they don't let scientists pick exactly where they insert the DNA. This means that the plant might change and grow in ways they can't predict. It's a faster way to breed plants than traditional crossbreeding, but it's not perfect.

The first genetically modified plants and animals were produced in the 1980s. In the 1990s, some products containing these foods started to appear on grocery shelves. For the most part, these products weren't different in a way that made a difference to consumers. They weren't tastier or more nutritious. Plants, for instance, had been changed to make them easier to grow. One common change made plants poisonous to damaging insects. Another change created plants that could survive after being sprayed with herbicides. That allowed farmers to kill weeds without killing their plants.

Once GM foods hit the stores, they weren't just a scientific experiment anymore. They were an everyday reality that made some people unhappy.

21st Century Content

Sometimes, one country will ban a food from another country because its leaders are concerned about safety. They might not want to purchase genetically modified food, or they might be worried that the food was not grown, shipped, or processed in a safe way. But sometimes, one country might ban a food for other reasons. It might want to protect its farmers by refusing to buy food from other countries or by charging very high taxes when it does. Or they might want to punish another country for doing something that they don't like. Decisions about which foods are sold are not always as simple as they might seem!

considering more than half of the world's genetically modified crops are grown in the United States. Roughly 60 percent of the processed food in the United States is made using genetically modified corn, soybeans, or canola!

In developing countries, there have been mixed feelings about genetically modified foods. Some countries are following the lead of European countries and banning most GM food. Leaders in other countries believe that GM foods can be a good way to feed their people, so they allow GM crops to be grown and sold.

Why are there such big differences between how people in different countries feel about GM food—especially in the United States versus European countries? That's a good question and one that's hard to answer. Some people might say it's because people in the United States don't take enough time to learn about important issues. Or it might be because Americans trust the government to only approve safe foods. Others think that Europeans are

The cereal in this bowl is an example of a processed food. The strawberries are fresh, or not processed.

more aware of issues that affect them or don't have as much trust in their leaders when it comes to food safety.

Other people argue that in Europe food has always been more than just "something to eat when we are hungry." Certain foods are part of each country's identity. They say that in the United States, where people from many different countries have settled, there is a mix of different foods. Because of this, there are few foods that are identified as American foods. These people think that this makes Americans more eager to try new methods for growing and processing food.

CHAPTER FOUR

IDEAS TAKE ROOT

*The farmer who planted these rice plants wants to get the
highest yield—as much rice as possible—from them.*

The discussion had certainly given the students a lot to sink their teeth
into! Dr. Ankur urged them to keep going.

"Let's list all the potentially good things we can think of about genetically modified foods," said Miyanda.

Scientists are always looking for ways to increase yield, which means getting more from a crop with the same amount of soil or seeds. They're also experimenting to see if they can create crops that will grow with less water or in poor soil. This could make it possible to grow food in areas that have problems with drought or don't have much good land for growing food.

Millions of the world's people don't have enough to eat, and the population is growing. The United Nations predicts that the world's population will grow to more than 9 billion by the year 2050. Some people think that GM foods will be needed to feed these people. Others say there's plenty of food in the world, but that politics and transportation problems stop it from getting to people who need it. There is no evidence that GM food will be able to solve the problem of world hunger. Even if it could, no one can say for sure that the foods would be safe enough. But scientists are working hard to try to find answers.

Some of the most common GM plants create their own toxins, or poisons, to kill harmful insects. Other genetic modifications help plants survive when certain chemicals are used to kill weeds. This means that farmers don't need to spray so many different kinds of chemicals or to spray them as often. Using fewer chemicals on crops helps protect the environment. Fewer chemicals enter the water system and the soil, and fewer chemicals are left on food. It also means that people who work on farms aren't exposed to as many chemicals.

GM foods could have another beneficial use. In some countries, it's hard to vaccinate people safely. There aren't always enough clean needles, and many vaccines have to be refrigerated—which is a luxury in some places. Some researchers think foods with vaccines built in could eliminate some of these problems. But they might cause others. For instance, it would be important to keep foods with vaccines separate from "normal" food of the same type. Also, doctors would have to make sure people got the complete dose of a vaccine.

Next, Miyanda asked the other students to list the potential problems of GM foods. Health problems were a big concern to the students.

"I guess we can't know for sure that genetically modified foods will be safe in the long run just because they've seemed safe so far," said Grace.

"But we have to remember, people who don't have enough food to feed their children tonight probably aren't too worried about whether something could hurt them 20 years from now," said Miyanda.

"People might be allergic to the GM foods," added Hiro.

"GM foods kill harmless insects," Charlie called out.

"They also hurt other plants," said Hiro.

"And poor farmers won't be able to afford the seeds," said Charlie.

✧ ✧ ✧

Testing is done to determine if a GM food has any known allergens. Companies aren't likely to use genes from foods that are known to cause allergies,

A man sprays pesticides on onion plants in Thailand. Plants that don't need pesticides can help workers avoid exposure to harmful chemicals.

like wheat or peanuts. Once, a company added a gene from the Brazil nut to soybeans to try to make them more nutritious. When they realized that

Some people are allergic to wheat which is found in bread and many other products. Researchers don't use foods known to cause allergies in GM food experiments.

many people were allergic to Brazil nuts, they stopped making the new soybean.

One study showed that monarch butterflies were more likely to die if they ate milkweed sprinkled with pollen from certain GM corn plants.

These GM plants had been altered with a gene from *Bacillus thuringiensis* (Bt). Bt is a bacteria in the soil that makes a poison that kills insects but doesn't hurt people. But some people believe this study wasn't accurate.

Genetic pollution is a big concern. This occurs when the pollen of a genetically modified plant is carried by wind, water, or an animal to another plant of the same species and cross-pollinates it. To prevent this, most farmers have a space called a buffer zone between their genetically modified plants and similar plants. The problem is that no one knows for sure just how big these buffer zones need to be. Sometimes changes have shown up even when plants were miles apart.

Large companies create most GM crops. This isn't too surprising because it can cost millions of dollars to research and test them. To pay for their investment, these companies usually sell their seeds for more money than regular seeds. Some companies also cover their cost by making farmers

21st Century Content

How can we be certain that GM foods are safe? We really can't. Although there haven't been any proven cases of GM foods causing health problems, they haven't been around long enough to prove they're completely safe either. How can we try to make food as safe as possible? One way is by having government rules that require companies to test their products. On the international level, the Codex Alimentarius Commission was set up to help countries work together to create standards for food safety.

Women in Zimbabwe plant corn seeds. Many farmers in developing countries save seeds from their plants to grow their next crop.

sign an agreement saying they won't save their seeds to plant a new crop. Farmers, especially those in developing countries, often rely on saved seeds to grow their next crop.

CHAPTER FIVE

HUNGRY TO LEARN MORE

Reading food labels is one way to be an educated consumer.

The conference had answered a lot of questions for the students—and gotten them thinking.

Grace wasn't convinced that GM foods were bad, but she realized she hadn't done enough in the past to be an educated consumer. She decided she'd write to each of the companies that made the processed foods she

In some countries, products that contain genetically modified foods must be labeled.

liked most—ice cream, pizza, and potato chips—and ask how they decided if the GM crops they used were safe.

Grace also wondered if it would be possible to label products in the United States like they do in England. She thought it was important for people to be able to make a choice about what they were eating. Maybe she would ask the companies she wrote to about that as well.

Grace planned to pay more attention to the land around the farms in her hometown. She'd never noticed if there were more weeds or fewer insects or animals by the GM crops. Now she would make a point of it.

While Charlie had always felt he knew a lot about GM foods, this conference raised some questions for him. "I guess there isn't necessarily anything bad that's been proven about genetically modified food, but I still don't know if I want to take any chances," he said.

But now Charlie could understand why it wasn't always easy to make a decision about using GM foods. If you were hungry today, it was pretty hard to worry about what might happen in the future.

For Miyanda, the best part of the conference was learning how science could make a difference in people's lives. The people of her country needed more safe, nutritious food. Maybe she could be one of the people who helped to make sure that they had it in the future. Miyanda didn't know if genetically modified foods would be the best choice for her country, but she knew that it was important to learn more about all of the options.

It's important for people from around the world to be involved in deciding how food will be produced in the future and which kinds of foods will be studied and grown. Farmers in developing countries don't usually grow crops that are popular in developed nations, such as wheat and corn, because of growing conditions or tradition. Some people worry that because the companies currently researching GM food are located in developed countries, only crops important to them will be produced. People from many different countries with many different opinions need to work together to make sure GM foods are regulated and safe.

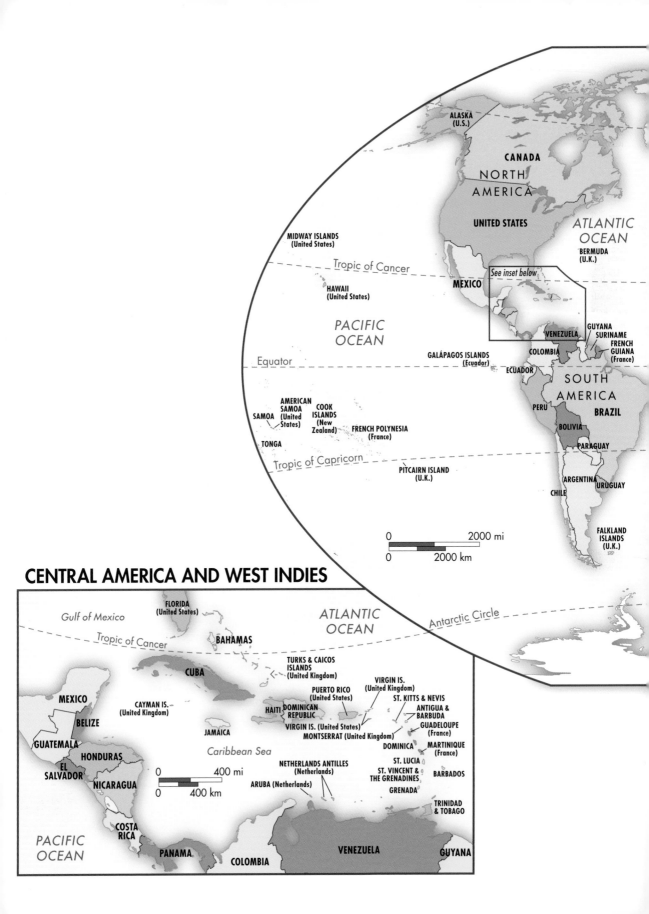

ALASKA
(U.S.)

CANADA

NORTH
AMERICA

ATLANTIC
OCEAN

UNITED STATES

BERMUDA
(U.K.)

MIDWAY ISLANDS
(United States)

Tropic of Cancer

MEXICO

See inset below

HAWAII
(United States)

PACIFIC
OCEAN

GUYANA
SURINAME
FRENCH
GUIANA
(France)

VENEZUELA

COLOMBIA

GALÁPAGOS ISLANDS
(Ecuador)

ECUADOR

Equator

SOUTH
AMERICA

PERU

BRAZIL

AMERICAN
SAMOA
(United
States)

COOK
ISLANDS
(New
Zealand)

BOLIVIA

SAMOA

FRENCH POLYNESIA
(France)

PARAGUAY

TONGA

Tropic of Capricorn

ARGENTINA

URUGUAY

PITCAIRN ISLAND
(U.K.)

CHILE

0   2000 mi

FALKLAND
ISLANDS
(U.K.)

0   2000 km

Antarctic Circle

CENTRAL AMERICA AND WEST INDIES

FLORIDA
(United States)

ATLANTIC
OCEAN

Gulf of Mexico

Tropic of Cancer

BAHAMAS

TURKS & CAICOS
ISLANDS
(United Kingdom)

CUBA

VIRGIN IS.
(United Kingdom)

MEXICO

CAYMAN IS.
(United Kingdom)

PUERTO RICO
(United States)

ST. KITTS & NEVIS

HAITI

DOMINICAN
REPUBLIC

ANTIGUA &
BARBUDA

BELIZE

GUADELOUPE
(France)

GUATEMALA

JAMAICA

VIRGIN IS. (United States)

MONTSERRAT (United Kingdom)

HONDURAS

Caribbean Sea

MARTINIQUE
(France)

EL
SALVADOR

DOMINICA

0   400 mi

ST. LUCIA

NICARAGUA

NETHERLANDS ANTILLES
(Netherlands)

ST. VINCENT &
THE GRENADINES

BARBADOS

0   400 km

ARUBA (Netherlands)

GRENADA

COSTA
RICA

PACIFIC
OCEAN

TRINIDAD
& TOBAGO

PANAMA

COLOMBIA

VENEZUELA

GUYANA

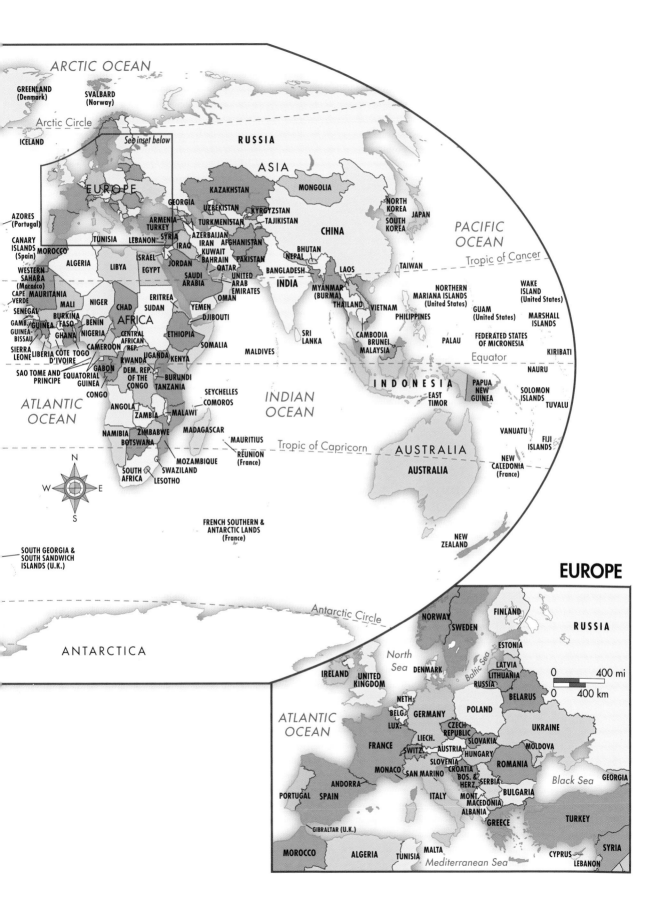

ARCTIC OCEAN

GREENLAND
(Denmark)

SVALBARD
(Norway)

Arctic Circle

ICELAND

RUSSIA

ASIA

AZORES
(Portugal)

EUROPE

See inset below

GEORGIA

CANARY
ISLANDS
(Spain)

MOROCCO

TUNISIA

ARMENIA
TURKEY

LEBANON

KAZAKHSTAN

UZBEKISTAN

TURKMENISTAN

SYRIA

AZERBAIJAN
IRAN
IRAQ

ISRAEL

KYRGYZSTAN

TAJIKISTAN

AFGHANISTAN

MONGOLIA

CHINA

NORTH
KOREA

SOUTH
KOREA

JAPAN

PACIFIC
OCEAN

Tropic of Cancer

WESTERN
SAHARA
(Morocco)

ALGERIA

LIBYA

EGYPT

JORDAN

KUWAIT

BAHRAIN

QATAR

SAUDI
ARABIA

PAKISTAN

BHUTAN

NEPAL

BANGLADESH

INDIA

UNITED
ARAB
EMIRATES

OMAN

MYANMAR
(BURMA)

LAOS

THAILAND

VIETNAM

TAIWAN

NORTHERN
MARIANA ISLANDS
(United States)

PHILIPPINES

GUAM
(United States)

WAKE
ISLAND
(United States)

MARSHALL
ISLANDS

CAPE
VERDE

MAURITANIA

MALI

NIGER

CHAD

ERITREA

SUDAN

YEMEN

DJIBOUTI

SENEGAL

GAMB.
GUINEA-
BISSAU

BURKINA
FASO

GUINEA

NIGERIA

BENIN

AFRICA

CENTRAL
AFRICAN
REP.

ETHIOPIA

SOMALIA

SRI
LANKA

MALDIVES

CAMBODIA

BRUNEI

MALAYSIA

PALAU

FEDERATED STATES
OF MICRONESIA

KIRIBATI

SIERRA
LEONE

GHANA

LIBERIA

CÔTE
D'IVOIRE

TOGO

CAMEROON

UGANDA

KENYA

Equator

NAURU

SAO TOME AND
PRINCIPE

EQUATORIAL
GUINEA

GABON

CONGO

RWANDA

DEM. REP.
OF THE
CONGO

BURUNDI

TANZANIA

INDONESIA

EAST
TIMOR

PAPUA
NEW
GUINEA

SOLOMON
ISLANDS

TUVALU

ATLANTIC
OCEAN

ANGOLA

ZAMBIA

MALAWI

SEYCHELLES

COMOROS

INDIAN
OCEAN

NAMIBIA

BOTSWANA

ZIMBABWE

MADAGASCAR

MAURITIUS

RÉUNION
(France)

Tropic of Capricorn

VANUATU

FIJI
ISLANDS

AUSTRALIA

AUSTRALIA

SOUTH
AFRICA

SWAZILAND

LESOTHO

MOZAMBIQUE

NEW
CALEDONIA
(France)

N

W   E

S

FRENCH SOUTHERN &
ANTARCTIC LANDS
(France)

NEW
ZEALAND

SOUTH GEORGIA &
SOUTH SANDWICH
ISLANDS (U.K.)

Antarctic Circle

ANTARCTICA

EUROPE

NORWAY

FINLAND

SWEDEN

RUSSIA

IRELAND

UNITED
KINGDOM

North
Sea

DENMARK

Baltic Sea

ESTONIA

LATVIA

LITHUANIA

RUSSIA

0   400 mi

0   400 km

BELARUS

NETH.

BELG.

LUX.

GERMANY

POLAND

UKRAINE

ATLANTIC
OCEAN

FRANCE

LIECH.

SWITZ.

CZECH
REPUBLIC

AUSTRIA

SLOVAKIA

HUNGARY

SLOVENIA

MOLDOVA

MONACO

SAN MARINO

CROATIA

BOS. &
HERZ.

ROMANIA

SERBIA

BLACK Sea

GEORGIA

ANDORRA

ITALY

MONT.

MACEDONIA

BULGARIA

PORTUGAL

SPAIN

ALBANIA

GREECE

TURKEY

GIBRALTAR (U.K.)

MOROCCO

ALGERIA

TUNISIA

MALTA

Mediterranean Sea

CYPRUS

SYRIA

LEBANON

GLOSSARY

allergens (AAH-lur-juhnss) substances that cause an allergy

bacterium (bak-TIHR-ee-uhm) a one-celled organism. Many cause disease; some can be used to help transfer genetic material.

chromosomes (KRO-muh-sohmss) structures inside a cell where DNA is found

crossbreeding (KRAWSS BREED-eeng) mixing different breeds of plants or animals

deoxyribonucleic acid (DNA) (dee-AHK-see-ri-bo-new-klay-ik ASS-id) a substance found in the cells of all living things that carries genetic information

enzyme (EN-zime) a form of protein that causes chemical changes in the body

genes (JEENZ) a section of DNA that passes along inherited characteristics from one generation of an organism to another

genetic (juh-NET-iks) having to do with characteristics that are passed from one generation to another

genetic modification (juh-NET-ik mod-uh-fih-KAY-shuhn) when a change is made to the genes of a living organism

genetically modified (GM) foods (juh-NET-ik-lee MOD-uh-fyed FOODZ) foods whose genes have been changed

herbicides (HUR-buh-sidez) chemicals used to kill weeds or other unwanted plants

organisms (OR-guh-niz-uhmz) living things. Plants, animals, and people are all organisms; so are one-celled bacteria.

processed food (PROSS-esst FOOD) food that is altered in some way from its natural state. An apple in the produce section is not a processed food; packaged cookies are.

protein (PROH-teen) chemicals in an organism created using instructions from the organism's genes. Proteins help the body to grow, change, and fix itself.

recombinant DNA (rDNA) (ree-KAHM-buh-nuhnt DEE EN AY) when DNA from two different organisms is combined

selection (suh-LEK-shuhn) a method of breeding living things that involves only growing or breeding the plants or animals that have desired characteristics

United Nations (yoo-NITE-id NAY-shuhns) a group made up of countries from around the world that was created after World War II to help countries work together

yield (YEELD) the amount of food that a plant produces

FOR MORE INFORMATION

Books

Freedman, Jeri. *Everything You Need to Know about Genetically Modified Foods*. New York: The Rosen Publishing Groups, Inc., 2003.

Morgan, Sally. *Superfoods: Genetic Modification of Foods*. Chicago: Heinemann Library, 2002.

Web Sites

Biotechnology Institute—What Is Biotechnology?
www.biotechinstitute.org/what_is
Discover more about the biotechnology industry

Greenpeace
www.greenpeace.org/usa/campaigns/genetic-engineering
Read about this organization's fight against GM foods

Monsanto
www.monsanto.com
Learn about the Monsanto company and how it uses biotechnology to develop new products

The U.S. Food and Drug Administration's Center for Food Safety and Applied Nutrition
www.cfsan.fda.gov
For information about many topics related to food safety and nutrition

INDEX

ABOUT THE AUTHOR

Vicky Franchino found it very interesting to learn more about the crops that many popular foods are made from. She had no idea so many foods were made from genetically-modified crops! Vicky is trying to become a better consumer and is paying more attention to the ingredients in her favorite foods. She is hopeful that scientists might one day find a way to make chocolate non-fattening. Vicky is the author of a number of other nonfiction books for children and lives with her husband and their three daughters in Wisconsin.